OKLAHOMA SOONERS

BY JIM GIGLIOTTI

Published by The Child's World®
1980 Lookout Drive • Mankato, MN 56003-1705
800-599-READ • www.childsworld.com

Copyright ©2022 by The Child's World®
All rights reserved. No part of this book may be reproduced or utilized in any form or by any means without written permission from the publisher.

Cover: Manny Flores/CSM/AP Images.
Interior: AP Images: Earl Shugars 9; Michael Ainsworth 13. Newscom: Ron Jenkins/KRT 10; Jon Soohoo/UPI 17; John Biever/Icon SMI 18; Matthew Pearce/Icon SMI 21. Wikimedia: 4, 6, 14 (Nmajdan)

ISBN 9781503850385 (Reinforced Library Binding)
ISBN 9781503850644 (Portable Document Format)
ISBN 9781503851405 (Online Multi-user eBook)
LCCN: 2021930293

Printed in the United States of America

Oklahoma players celebrate another big play for the Sooners.

CONTENTS

Why We Love College Football   4

CHAPTER ONE
Early Days   7

CHAPTER TWO
Glory Years   8

CHAPTER THREE
Best Year Ever!   11

CHAPTER FOUR
Oklahoma Traditions   12

CHAPTER FIVE
Meet the Mascot   15

CHAPTER SIX
Top Oklahoma QBs   16

CHAPTER SEVEN
Other Oklahoma Heroes   19

CHAPTER EIGHT
Recent Superstars   20

Glossary   22

Find Out More   23

Index   24

WHY WE LOVE COLLEGE FOOTBALL

It's time for college football! The leaves are changing color. Happy crowds fill the stadiums. Pennants wave. And here come the fight songs! College football is one of America's most popular sports. Millions of fans follow their favorite teams. They wear school colors and hope for big wins.

That long line of "O's" are not zeros . . . they are the start of an O-O-O-Oklahoma chant!

The University of Oklahoma is one of college football's best. Its long history includes lots of championships. Great players have worn the crimson and cream. Let's meet the famous Sooners!

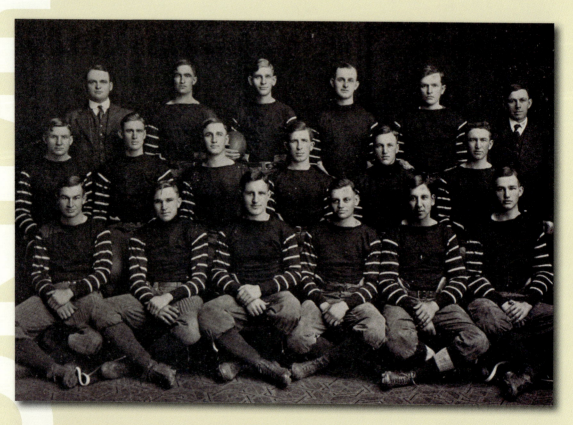

Above: Running back Forest Geyer (top row, third from left) was an All-America for the undefeated 1915 Sooners.

CHAPTER ONE

Early Days

The University of Oklahoma has been playing football since 1895. That is longer than Oklahoma has been a state! Oklahoma did not become the 46th state until 1907.

Their first season, the team lost the only game it played. In 1915, the Sooners won all 10 of their games. They have gone unbeaten in nine seasons since.

They didn't have another **losing season** until 1922. Bennie Owen was the team's first great coach. The field at the team's home stadium is named in his honor.

> ## WHAT'S A SOONER?
> Oklahoma's nickname comes from the state's **pioneer** days. The Oklahoma Territory was opened in 1889. Some settlers tried to get a head start to claim land. They went too soon. Those settlers were called "Sooners."

CHAPTER TWO

Glory Years

Oklahoma football has nearly always been very good. The Sooners played their 126th season in 2020. They had a winning record for the 104th time. Since 1945, Oklahoma has won the most games in college football.

For a time in the 1950s, Oklahoma was unbeatable! They were led by coach Bud Wilkinson. The Sooners won 47 games in a row from 1953 to1957. That is the longest winning streak in college football history (among the top-division teams). They won three national titles in that time.

Oklahoma added two more national championships in the 1970s and one in the '80s. The Sooners won their most recent title in 2000.

After another win on their long streak, the Sooners carried ➤
coach Bud Wilkinson off the field in triumph.

CHAPTER THREE

Best Year Ever!

It's hard to pick the best year from so many great seasons. Oklahoma has been so good for so long.

In 2000, Oklahoma went 13–0. Six of its wins came over **ranked** opponents. The Sooners beat No. 1 Nebraska and No. 2 Kansas State.

The 2000 Sooners were packed with talent. Quarterback Josh Heupel passed for 3,606 yards to lead the offense. He was

GOING BOWLING

Oklahoma has played in dozens of bowl games. In 2020, the team blasted Florida 55–20 in the Cotton Bowl. That was Oklahoma's 22nd bowl game in a row.

a first-team **All-America** pick. Linebacker Rocky Calmus and safety J.T. Thatcher were All-Americas on defense. Together, they helped Oklahoma win the national championship.

Left, Josh Heupel led Oklahoma to a great start in 2000. The team scored at least 30 points in nine straight games!

CHAPTER FOUR

Oklahoma Traditions

"Boomer Sooner!" The sound echoes over Oklahoma's stadium. "Boomer!" the fans on one side shout. "Sooner!" yells back the other side. The "Boomer Sooner!" cheers go back and forth. The sound grows as the team runs onto the field!

THE BIG RIVAL!

Oklahoma's biggest **rival is** the University of Texas. Their **Big 12** game is called the Red River Showdown. The Red River separates the two states. The teams first played each other in 1900.

The cheer is also the name of the school's fight song. "Boomer Sooner" is played after every first down and touchdown . . . and lots of times in between. Sooners fans love it! Opposing teams, well, not so much.

Right, Spencer Rattler (7) celebrates with T.J. Pledger (5) after the running back scored in the 2020 Red River Showdown.

CHAPTER FIVE

Meet the Mascot

The Sooner Schooner races onto the field during home games. It is a wagon pulled by horses. The Schooner drives out before every game and after every Oklahoma touchdown. The crowd goes wild! Oklahoma pioneers used a similar wagon in the late 1800s.

OKLAHOMA MEMORIAL STADIUM

Oklahoma plays in Gaylord Family Oklahoma Memorial Stadium. Usually that's shortened to Memorial Stadium! Visiting teams have it tough. The Sooners won 39 games in a row at home from 2005–11.

The white ponies that pull the Sooner Schooner are named Boomer and Sooner, of course. A student group called the RUF/NEKs runs the Sooner Schooner. The RUF/NEKs have been around for more than 100 years. They are the oldest male spirit club in America.

Steered by students and pulled by white horses, the Sooner Schooner speeds down the field!

15

CHAPTER SIX

Top Oklahoma QBs

In the 2000s, Oklahoma has had some great quarterbacks. Josh Heupel started the run of success. He led the team to the 2000 national title. Three years later, Jason White won the Heisman Trophy. That is given to college football's best player.

Sam Bradford set a school record for passing yards in a season in 2008. He won the Heisman, too. In 2017 and 2018, Baker Mayfield and Kyler Murray gave the Sooners back-to-back Heisman quarterbacks. All three passers were No. 1 picks in the NFL Draft, too.

> **WISHBONE QBS**
>
> In the 1970s and 1980s, Oklahoma's offense ran the wishbone. In this style of play, the QB runs a lot. Steve Davis, Tomas Lott, and Jamelle Holieway were wishbone QB stars.

Right, Baker Mayfield set a Sooners record with 131 passing touchdowns. He played for Oklahoma from 2013 to 2017. ➤

CHAPTER SEVEN

Other Oklahoma Heroes

In 1952, Billy Vessels was the Sooners' first Heisman winner. Steve Owens won the award in 1969. Billy Sims won it in 1978. All three were running backs.

You have to play great defense to win as many titles as the Sooners. Lucious Selmon was an All-America on the defensive line in 1973. His younger brothers Lee Roy and

ALL-AMERICA TEAM

In 1913, fullback Claude Reed was the Sooners' first All-America. The school's total is now up to 167. That is the most of any school in the nation.

Dewey were All-Americas, too. Brian Bosworth is the only player ever to win the Butkus Award twice (1985–86). That trophy goes to college football's top linebacker.

◄ *Brian Bosworth scowls at the other team's quarterback. The fierce linebacker was one of the best tacklers ever.*

CHAPTER EIGHT

Recent Superstars

The Sooners won at least 10 games nine times during the 2010s. Bob Stoops and Lincoln Riley coached many top players.

Those Sooners teams featured great receivers. Ryan Broyles, Dede Westbrook, Marquise Brown, and CeeDee Lamb were All-Americas in the 2010s.

It was not just receivers, though. In 2014, running back Samaje Perine gained a record 427 yards in a one game! In 2017, Mark Andrews won the Mackey Award. That trophy goes to the nation's best **tight end**.

Spencer Rattler passed for 3,031 yards and 28 touchdowns in 2020. Will he be the Sooners' next great quarterback?

Right: In only his first year as a starter, Spencer Rattler ►
led the Big 12 in passing yards and TD passes.

GLOSSARY

All-America (ALL uh-MAYR-ih-kuh) an honor given to players that experts consider the best players in a given year

Big 12 (BIG TWELVE) the name of the conference, or group of teams, in which the Sooners play a yearly schedule of games

losing season (LOO–zing SEE-zun) a season in which a team has fewer wins than losses

pioneer (pye-uh-NEER) one of the first settlers in a territory

ranked (RANKT) included on a national list of top college football teams

rival (RYE-vul) an individual or team that competes for the same thing

tight end (TYTE END) an offensive position that catches passes and blocks

FIND OUT MORE

IN THE LIBRARY

Fishman, Jon M. *Baker Mayfield*. Minneapolis, MN: *Lerner Publishing Group, 2021.*

Jacobs, Greg. *Everything Football Kids!* New York, NY: Adams Media, 2019.

Rowland, Toby. *Unhitch the Wagon: The Story of Boomer and Sooner*. Overland Park, KS: Ascend Books, 2020.

Weber, Margaret. *Oklahoma Sooners*. New York, NY: Weigl, 2020.

ON THE WEB

Visit our website for links about the
Oklahoma Sooners:
childsworld.com/links

Note to Parents, Teachers, and Librarians: We routinely verify our Web links to make sure they are safe and active sites. So encourage your readers to check them out!

INDEX

Andrews, Mark 20
"Boomer Sooner," 12, 15
Bosworth, Brian 19
Bradford, Sam 16
Broyles, Ryan 20
Calmus, Rocky 11
Cotton Bowl 11
Florida 11
Gaylord Family Oklahoma Memorial Stadium 15
Geyer, Forest 6
Heisman Trophy 16, 19
Heupel, Josh 11, 16
Kansas State 11
Lamb, CeeDee 20
Mayfield, Baker 16
Murray, Kyler 16
Nebraska 11
Owen, Bennie 7
Owens, Steve 19
Perine, Samaje 20
Pledger, T.J. 12
Rattler, Spencer 12, 20
Red River Showdown 12
Reed, Claude 19
Riley, Lincoln 20
RUF/NEKS 15
Selmon, Dewey 19
Selmon, Lee Roy 19
Selmon, Lucious 19
Sooner Schooner 15
Stoops, Bob 20
Texas 12
Thatcher, J.T. 11
Vessels, Billy 19
Westbrook, Dede 20
White, Jason 16
Wilkinson, Bud 8

ABOUT THE AUTHOR

Jim Gigliotti has written more than 100 books
for young readers, many of them on sports.
He attended the University of Southern California and
worked in the athletic department for the Trojans—
another of college football's best teams!